# MERRY CHRISTMAS
# Mr. Snowman

**(The Snowman's Christmas Present)**

*Story and Illustrations by* IRMA WILDE

Wonder® Books
**PRICE/STERN/SLOAN**
*Publishers, Inc., Los Angeles*
**1983**

*THIS is the story that the Snowman told to the Big Red Sun at sunset on Christmas Day:*

Three children made a Snowman yesterday while
the snowflakes were still falling. And I am the Snowman that they made.

Billy, the oldest child, gave me my nose. It's that nice orange carrot you see. Mary found two lumps of coal for my eyes, and little Davey drew my mouth with a stick. My mouth drooped at the corners a bit because Davey is too little to draw very well.

"Tomorrow is Christmas," said Billy. "I hope Santa Claus brings me a sled, a ball, a bike and a puppy."

"Me too," said little Davey. "Me too!"

"I want a doll that looks like a princess, a handbag, a dress and a doll carriage to wheel. Oh, I wish it was Christmas right now!" said Mary.

"Me too!" cried Billy.

"Me too!" cried little Davey. "Me too!"

They laughed and ran around and around the yard, and their cheeks were bright with the cold. And all the time the snowflakes were still falling.

It was quiet in the yard when the children had gone,
and I was left there alone. My mouth had melted a bit
and drooped even more at the corners.

The shadows grew longer and the day went to sleep.
The snow clouds blew away and the stars came out in
the deep dark sky.

There were lights in the windows, and I could see Billy and Mary and little Davey trimming the Christmas tree. "Put a red ball here and a blue ball there," cried Billy. "And a lovely angel on the very tiptop," laughed Mary. "Oh, I wish Christmas Day would hurry and come!" "Me too!" cried little Davey. "Me too!"

"Now we must go to bed and shut our eyes and wish very hard for Christmas. Then, while we're asleep, Santa will come. And when we wake up—why, it will be Christmas!" said Billy to Mary and little Davey.

So they went to bed and they fell asleep. All the lights in the house went out, and the night slept, too. I felt very lonely.

Suddenly, far away up in the stars, I heard a tinkling and a jingling that sounded like bells. And a wonderful sight came out of the dark sleepy night!

It was SANTA CLAUS!

He was riding in a sleigh loaded down with toys. It
was pulled by eight reindeer, and they ran like the wind.
The tinkling of the sleigh bells filled the night, and
the starlight sparkled on Santa and the eight reindeer.

They stopped on the roof top, and Santa whisked
down the chimney.

Soon Santa had left all the presents piled around
the dark shining Christmas tree.

Then the most wonderful thing happened. And it happened to me! Santa reached down and picked up the stick little Davey had dropped near my feet.

"There now," he said a few minutes later, "even a Snowman must know Santa loves him." And he rode away in the dark starry night.

Early this morning the children ran into the yard.
"Merry Christmas, Mr. Snowman!" they shouted.

Then they were quiet and filled with wonder. There
I was, standing proudly, with my Christmas presents.

For I wore Santa's very own cap, his nice woolly red cap—a gift just for me from Santa Claus.

But Santa had given me another wonderful present, too. Little Davey noticed it right away.

"Look!" he cried, pointing. And sure enough, gone from my face was the drooping mouth little Davey had drawn. Santa Claus had given me a big broad happy smile—the finest Christmas present in the world!

Everyone was glad the Snowman had not been for-
gotten on Christmas Day! And everyone smiled a happy
Christmas smile just like the one Santa gave me!

*And the Big Red Sun was happy, too.*